D0431922

Soto, Gary.
Chato goes cruisin'
p2008, c2005.
33305802610430
ca   02/13/09

GARY SOTO

CHATO GOES CRUISIN'

ILLUSTRATED BY
SUSAN GUEVARA

G. P. PUTNAM'S SONS

crunch
a bunch

WIN!

"Win a Cruise for Two!" Chato read while popping crunchies into his mouth. Feeling lucky, he clawed the entry form from the bag.

A few weeks later, Chato shouted, "¡*Chihuahua!*
We won!"

"Won what, homecat?" Novio Boy asked.

"The Cruise for Two!" Chato became dreamy.

MAN, I'VE ALWAYS WANTED TO TASTE COCONUT MILK.

PLUS EAT FISH TACOS *EN LA PLAYA*.

AND THERE'S A LOT OF SAND FOR YOU-KNOW-WHAT.

They giggled and gave each other a low-four.

When they arrived at the dock, they were surprised to find it full of dogs. Two huskies large as couches were running up the gangplank. A Chihuahua was shivering and barking on the deck.

"I don't know about this," Novio Boy cried.

"Come on . . . they look like nice *perritos*," Chato pleaded.

Novio Boy knew that his best friend wanted to go on the cruise real bad. He would do it for Chato! After all, they had known each other since they were kittens. Best friends, they even shared the same water bowl.

"*Pues*, I guess I can hang," Novio Boy said bravely.

"Welcome aboard, my feline *amigos*," the captain called.

The first night, dinner was canned dog food in a fancy taco shell, plus sixteen kinds of dog biscuits.

"How can they eat this grub?" Novio Boy whispered. He breathed into his paws, picking up a peculiar odor.

"You got any gum?" Chato asked. He rolled his tongue over his fangs. "This *comida* is *fuchi*."

Under the stars, the dogs partied down. They played Jump for the Frisbee, Tree the Cat, and Pitch the Flea Collar. When they started to dance the Hound Dog Hustle, Chato and Novio Boy were swatted by the tails of wild partying dogs.

"They play rough," Chato remarked.

"And they don't have any games for us," Novio Boy meowed sadly.

The two friends went to bed. Unable to sleep because the dogs kept howling, Chato and Novio Boy slinked down to the library.

In the morning, Chato planned to snooze in the sun. But the dogs had taken over the deck, running around with their faces fat with Milk-Bones.

The next day, Chato and Novio Boy played with tangled yarn and a chewed-up tennis ball. They batted around a cloth rat until they were bored, bored, bored. Then they made up their own game called Scaredy Cat. Chato and Novio Boy hopped onto the ship's rail.

"Takes *purrrrr*fect cat balance," Chato sang.

"*Fíjate*. Check me out," Novio Boy bragged. "One *pata* and I ain't even using my nails to hang on."

On the third day, the captain barked on the loudspeaker,
"Attention, please. We have a medical emergency! But don't panic."
He staggered toward Chato and Novio Boy. "The dogs are sick and
the radio's broken. Take the rowboat," he said weakly. "Get help."

S. BARRY

Chato and Novio Boy were happy to get off the cruise ship.

"We'll be back," they promised.

The two cats rowed like mad for hours and hours. Their arms ached before they spotted a ship.

"¡Mira!" Chato shouted. "It's a cat cruise, the one we should have been on."

The partying cats were wild as pirates. They were *loco* on catnip and fat from drinking bottles of milk. They had bags under their eyes from staying up all night.

"Ahoy!" Chato yelled. "¡Ayudanos! Help us, friends! A whole shipload of dogs is sick."

"Don't worry about them. They're only dogs," an orange cat yelled. "Party with us."

Although it sounded like a cool time, they had given their word to the captain. They had to find help for the dogs.

"We gave our *palabra*, homecat," Chato said. "We gotta keep going."

The two cats paddled away. Away and away until the sky darkened, the wind roared, and the waves grew large and wicked.

Be brave, Chato told himself. But he closed his eyes when the really big waves splashed them.

Suddenly, their rowboat was lifted onto a huge wave that sent them head over tail . . .

. . . onto a soft, sandy beach. They were both wet as mops, and Novio Boy had lost his earring.

But they were glad to be alive, and extra glad because now they found themselves among vacationing veterinarians!

¡OYE! THERE'S THESE SICK DOGS THAT NEED SOME PILLS OR SOMETHING.

YOU DON'T LOOK TOO WELL YOURSELVES.

Bzz Bz Psst Bzzz

VETS TO THE RESCUE!

In no time they were on board the dog cruise ship. The vets got to work on the poor pooches, who whined and howled.

"I hate it when they put that stick in your mouth." Chato gagged.

"Or when they shine that light in your eyes," Novio Boy agreed. "It's like the headlights of a car."

"Like you're going to get run over, huh?" Chato remarked.

When Chato and Novio Boy got home, their legs were wobbly from living on a cruise ship for a week. They staggered around and fell. They laughed as they remembered when they were kittens and could hardly walk.

Novio Boy brought out a brand-new bag of his favorite cat food. "Finally," he said, "real food."

He read: "Win a Cruise to the Canary Islands!"

"*Orale,*" Chato meowed and gave his friend a low-four. "But this time we get on the right boat."

The two friends sailed to the mailbox, cruising the street slow and easy.

Glossary

agua water

amigos friends

¡Ayudanos! Help us!

¡Chihuahua! Oh, wow!

comida food

el barrio the neighborhood

en la playa at the beach

fíjate look at this

fuchi stinky, yucky

loco crazy

¡Lonche! Lunch!

¡Mira! Look!

muy very

¡No problema! No problem!

orale all right

¡Oye! Listen to me!

pachanga festive party

palabra word

pata paw

perritos little dogs

pues well

tú sabes you know

un gato a cat

To Mariko, our own private vet. —G.S.

Mil gracias, AIR Head Productions, and La I.G. también! —S.G.

G. P. PUTNAM'S SONS

A division of Penguin Young Readers Group. Published by The Penguin Group.

PENGUIN GROUP (USA) INC., 345 Hudson Street, New York, NY 10014, U.S.A. PENGUIN GROUP (CANADA), 10 Alcorn Avenue, Toronto, Ontario, Canada M4V 3B2 (a division of Pearson Penguin Canada Inc.) PENGUIN BOOKS LTD, 80 Strand, London WC2R 0RL, England. PENGUIN IRELAND, 25 St. Stephen's Green, Dublin 2, Ireland (a division of Penguin Books Ltd.) PENGUIN BOOKS INDIA PVT LTD, 11 Community Centre, Panchsheel Park, New Delhi - 110 017, India. PENGUIN GROUP (NZ), Cnr Airborne and Rosedale Roads, Albany, Auckland, New Zealand (a division of Pearson New Zealand Ltd). PENGUIN BOOKS (SOUTH AFRICA) (PTY) LTD, 24 Sturdee Avenue, Rosebank, Johannesburg 2196, South Africa. PENGUIN BOOKS LTD, Registered Offices: 80 Strand, London WC2R 0RL, England.

Text copyright © 2005 by Gary Soto. Illustrations copyright © 2005 by Susan Guevara. All rights reserved.

This book, or parts thereof, may not be reproduced in any form without permission in writing from the publisher, G. P. Putnam's Sons, a division of Penguin Young Readers Group, 345 Hudson Street, New York, NY 10014. G. P. Putnam's Sons, Reg. U.S. Pat. & Tm. Off. The scanning, uploading and distribution of this book via the Internet or via any other means without the permission of the publisher is illegal and punishable by law. Please purchase only authorized electronic editions, and do not participate in or encourage electronic piracy of copyrighted materials. Your support of the author's rights is appreciated. Published simultaneously in Canada. Manufactured in China by South China Printing Co. Ltd. Design by Cecilia Yung. Text set in 14-point Meridien Medium. The full-color art was done in acrylic on scratchboard. The black-and-white comic strips were done in black ink on bristol board.

Library of Congress Cataloging-in-Publication Data Soto, Gary. Chato goes cruisin' / Gary Soto ; illustrated by Susan Guevara. p. cm. Summary: Chato and Novio Boy win a cruise but are disappointed to find that everyone else on board is a dog, and things go from bad to worse when the dogs party themselves sick and it is up to the cats to find help. [1. Cruise ships—Fiction. 2. Loyalty—Fiction. 3. Promises—Fiction. 4. Sick—Fiction. 5. Cats—Fiction. 6. Dogs—Fiction. 7. Mexican Americans—Fiction.] I. Guevara, Susan, ill. II. Title: Chato goes cruising. III. Title. PZ7.S7242Cg 2005 [E]—dc22 2003012741 ISBN 0-399-23974-X

3 5 7 9 10 8 6 4